The Gingerbread Rabbit

Michael di Capua Books

HarperCollins Publishers

The Gingerbread Rabbit

By RANDALL JARRELL

Pictures by Garth Williams

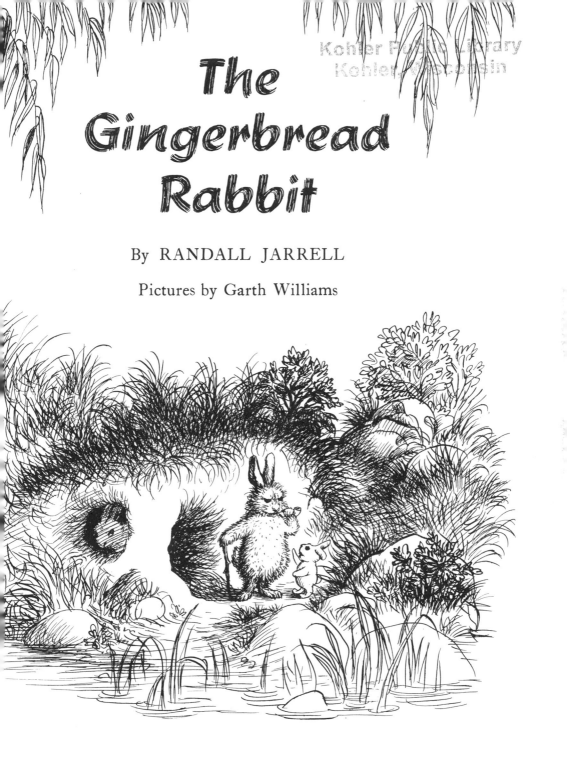

to my little Mary

Once upon a time there was a mother with only one child. She loved the little girl so much that one morning, after she'd seen her off to school, she sat down in the kitchen by the fire and said to herself: "What can I do for a surprise for my little Mary, this afternoon when she comes home?"

At first she couldn't think of anything, but as she sat staring out the window she saw hop from behind a bush, right on the edge of the forest, the biggest, brownest rabbit she'd ever seen. She went over to the door, opened it a little, and peeped out at him. The rabbit saw her, but instead of running away he just looked at her. She tiptoed toward him a step at a time, until finally she could almost reach out and touch him, and still the rabbit didn't

1

stir. But all of a sudden he wrinkled up his nose, twitched his ears, and gave a big sneeze. It was such a big sneeze that it made the mother jump, and the rabbit jumped too, and away he went into the forest.

The mother said to herself: "Never in all my life have I seen a rabbit as big as that or as brown as that or as tame as that—what a pity he won't be here this afternoon for my little girl to see!" And no sooner had she said it than she thought of the surprise she could have for her daughter. She went back into the kitchen, got out some flour and molasses and brown sugar and ginger, mixed them together in a mixing bowl, and rolled them out on the kitchen table with a rolling pin. It all smelled so good the mother couldn't keep from licking the spoon. Then she took a paring knife, and with it she cut out of the dough a big brown gingerbread rabbit. He had on trousers that came down to his knees and a coat that came up to his neck; and the mother took two

raisins and stuck them on his face for eyes, and a cherry for his mouth, and a big blanched almond for his nose—and somehow, when she'd finished the gingerbread rabbit, he looked exactly like the real rabbit she'd seen at the edge of the forest.

Just as the mother was about to put the rabbit into the oven she heard, from out in front of the house, something that went *clop-clop*, and then went *creak-creak*, and then called out in a low, slow, squeaky voice:

"Turnip greens, fresh turnip greens!
  Carrots and corn on the cob and beans,
  Black-eyed peas just picked today—
  If you don't come buy 'em
  I'll throw 'em away."

It was the vegetable man's horse and the vegetable man's wagon and the vegetable man. So the mother left the gingerbread rabbit on the table, went into the front yard, and picked out some vegetables for dinner that night. But they looked so fresh and smelled so good that she got some for the next day and the day after that—it took her a long time to pick out everything she wanted.

While she was gone the gingerbread rabbit lay there on the kitchen table, and the morning sun streamed in through the window and fell on his coat and trousers. After a while the sunshine warmed them so and dried them so that they had a lovely look and smell, like clothes someone has just ironed. The sunshine fell on the rabbit's arms and legs too, and warmed them and dried them till they looked just lovely, like a puppy's legs after he's been given a bath and wrapped in a towel and put in front of the fire to dry. And the sunshine fell on the raisins that were the rabbit's eyes, and the cherry that was his mouth, and the almond that was his nose—and each of them got warmer and warmer and drier and drier, until at last the rabbit blinked his eyes, licked his lips, and wrinkled his nose. And then, all at once, he gave a big sneeze. He hopped to his feet, looked around him, and said: "Where am I?"

"Here in the kitchen," said the paring knife.

"What's a kitchen?" said the rabbit.

"It's where they cook you and eat you," said the paring knife.

"Me?" said the rabbit.

"You," said the paring knife.

"What do they want to eat me for?" said the rabbit. He sounded frightened.

"Because you're a rabbit," said the mixing bowl.

"What's a rabbit?" said the rabbit.

"It's an animal that lives in the forest," said the mixing bowl, "and whenever anyone comes near him he runs away, because he's afraid they'll shoot him and eat him."

"They're going to *shoot* me?" said the rabbit.

"Oh no, not you," said the paring knife. "You're only a gingerbread rabbit. They'll put you in the oven and bake you."

"In the oven and *bake* me?" said the rabbit. He sounded more frightened than ever.

"Yes, bake you!" said the rolling pin. "Bake you and eat you!"

The rabbit said: "I don't want them to bake me! I don't want them to eat me!"

The paring knife and the mixing bowl and the rolling pin all laughed. "It makes no difference what you want," said the rolling pin. "In a minute the woman will come in and pick you up and put you in the oven, and that will be the end of you."

"Maybe I can hide," said the rabbit.

"A rabbit your size!" said the rolling pin. "Just look at yourself."

The rabbit looked at the ends of his arms and the ends of his legs, and they did look a long way off from his head. When he looked at himself in the spoon that was on the table he looked smaller, but he looked all blurred too, with his legs at the top and his head at the bottom. He didn't like that, so he looked at

himself in the side of the pan. He looked as
blurred as ever, but all thin and curved and
queer. He looked away as fast as he could, and
then he saw himself in the glass of the window
—there was a shutter behind part of it, so that
it reflected him just as if it were a mirror.
"Why, I'm beautiful," said the rabbit.

"Beautiful!" said the mixing bowl. "Why, you're not even round."

"Beautiful!" said the rolling pin. "Why, you're not even wooden."

"Beautiful!" said the paring knife. "Why, you're not even a paring knife."

The rabbit didn't hear them, but just kept on staring at himself in the glass. "How brown I am!" he said to the others. "How round and red my mouth is, and how crinkly my eyes are, and what a slender delicate nose I have. You've got to admit it would be a terrible thing to eat a nose like that."

"They eat them all the time," said the paring knife. "The woman eats them, and her husband eats them, and her little girl eats them. Everything that comes into this kitchen they eat."

The rabbit said: "Are they going to eat you?"

"Oh no," said the paring knife in a complacent voice. "*We're* not edible."

"It doesn't seem to me that I'm edible," said the rabbit wistfully.

Said the rolling pin: "Wait and see!"

The rabbit said to the mixing bowl: "You said that out in the forest, whenever anyone comes near a rabbit, the rabbit runs away."

"That's right," said the mixing bowl. "He's afraid they'll eat him."

"Then *I'll* run away," the rabbit said. "*I'm* afraid they'll eat me."

"Everything that comes into this kitchen," repeated the paring knife, "they eat."

"Nothing has ever got away," said the mixing bowl.

"Nothing!" said the paring knife.

"Maybe if I begged them not to eat me," said the rabbit.

The paring knife and the mixing bowl and the rolling pin laughed. Then they heard the front door open. "She's coming! She's coming!" said all three of them. The rabbit hopped back across the table and lay down flat, but he held his head cater-cornered so he could see the door out of the corner of his eye. He was so frightened that half the time he couldn't breathe—the other half of the time he took such big breaths that he shook all over.

The door opened and in came a tremendous giant with her arms full of paper sacks, each of them so big she could have stuffed the rabbit inside. Her arms were four times the size of the rabbit's and her legs were eight times the size of the rabbit's, and instead of her having a cherry for a mouth, there in the middle of her face were dozens of tremendous shining white teeth the size of a grizzly bear's. That was how she looked to the rabbit. "I haven't a *chance*," thought the rabbit.

The mother put down the sacks, went over to the stove and opened the oven door, and said out loud: "My goodness, those vegetables took a long time. I must get the gingerbread in the oven right away."

When the rabbit heard her say this he

thought: "It's so, it's all so. They're really going to bake me! They're really going to eat me!" The giant walked across the room and bent down over him, and her teeth glittered in the sunlight. Just as she was about to pick him up she said to herself: "Oh my, what with all these sacks I didn't even close the front door. I'd better go back and shut it."

The rabbit's heart beat faster, and he gave a sigh of relief. But then the mother said to the rabbit, giving him a little pat: "No, I'll just put you in the oven first and then I'll shut the door." She picked up the rabbit and started across to the oven with him, but he gave a squeal of terror, wriggled out of her hands, ran across the kitchen, and disappeared through the kitchen door. The mother was so surprised she didn't know what to do, but then she ran into the living room just in time to see the rabbit rush out the front door.

"Stop! Stop!" cried the mother. The rabbit didn't say a word, but ran for the forest as fast as his legs would carry him. His legs stuck out underneath him, and his arms stuck out at both sides, and his ears stuck out on top, and he ran so fast that whenever he'd lose his balance and start to fall down, he'd roll over and over like a wheel with six spokes. He rolled faster than he ran, even—you couldn't tell

which were his legs or which were his arms or which were his ears, they went around and around so fast.

Down the path into the forest the rabbit ran, and after him ran the mother, calling: "Come back! Come back!" At first the rabbit ran so much faster than the mother that he got way ahead—the mother couldn't even see him any more, there were so many trees in between. But then the rabbit began to pant a little, and then he panted a lot, and then he panted so hard he shook all over. He ran a little slower to try to get his breath, and then instead of running he hopped, and then instead of hopping he walked. The mother would surely have caught him, but she began to get out of breath too, and instead of running she trotted, and then instead of trotting she walked. When the rabbit would get to a sunny spot he'd pant and fan himself and wish he could sit down and rest; and behind him the mother would come to a shady spot, and she'd get her breath

back a little and give a big sigh of relief and
go on a little faster. But by then the rabbit
would have got to a shady spot, and he'd feel
cooler and get his breath back a little and go

on a little faster; and then the mother would come to the sunny spot and pant and fan herself and wish she could sit down and rest. Every once in a while the mother would stop for a second and hear the rabbit's footsteps in the leaves ahead, and then she'd start on after him; and every once in a while the rabbit would stop and hear the mother's footsteps behind him, and he'd say to himself: "She's after me! She's after me! I just can't keep on running—if only I could hide!"

Just then the path came to a tremendous oak tree and divided in two: half the path disappeared into the forest on the left and the other half disappeared into the forest on the right. Up in the oak tree there sat a big gray squirrel, holding in his mouth a leafy green branch. In a minute he ran along the oak tree bough, with the green branch trailing behind him like a flag. And then he came to where there was a big pile of leaves and branches in a fork of the tree, most of them old brown dried-out leaves but a few of them new green ones. He stuffed the new branch in with all the others. This was the squirrel's nest. Every night he'd burrow inside it (the way you get down inside the bedclothes when you go to bed on a cold night) and then, even if it rained or hailed or snowed, the squirrel would be warm and dry in the middle of all the leaves.

As soon as the rabbit saw the squirrel's nest he thought: "She'd never catch me there." So he called up: "Squirrel!"

"Yes?" said the squirrel.

"There's a giant chasing me that's going to cook me and eat me," said the rabbit. "I've run and I've run till I just can't run any more. If you'll let me hide in your nest I'll be so grateful to you that I'll—"

"Yes?" said the squirrel.

"Well, I don't really know anything I can do for you," said the rabbit, "but I'll be *so* grateful."

"I'd let you hide in my nest," said the

squirrel, "but what good will it do? The giant will just reach up and pull you out."

"Oh, she's not that big a giant," said the rabbit. "She'll never be able to reach that high. And besides, I'll get right in the middle of your nest and she'll never see me. Please let me! Please let me!"

"All right," said the squirrel. "Come on up!"

"But I *can't* come up," the rabbit said. "I can't climb, I'm only a rabbit. If you'll come down to the end of the bough and reach down as far as you can, I'll jump as high as I can and catch on to you, and then you can pull me up on the bough."

"All right," said the squirrel. He ran along the bough till he came to the end of it, sank his claws into the bark, and reached down as far as he could. The rabbit jumped as high as he could, caught hold of the squirrel's paws, and plop! they both fell down head over heels —the rabbit was too heavy for the squirrel.

"It's no use," said the rabbit. "I'm just too big."

"We can try over," the squirrel said. "This time I'll—"

But at that moment they heard the footsteps coming through the leaves. "Good-by," said the rabbit. "I'll go this way and maybe the giant will go the other way. Thank you *so* much, squirrel." And he started down the path to the right—then he called back over his shoulder: "Hide! Hide!"

The squirrel ran up the trunk of the oak tree as fast as he could go, and bounded out to his nest in three jumps; then he burrowed down inside it as far as he could go. He heard the giant's footsteps getting louder and louder, and then all of a sudden they stopped. For a minute there wasn't a sound. Then something gave a big sob, and another big sob, and began to cry as if its heart would break. The squirrel thought: "The giant's *crying*." He crept over to the edge of the leaves and peeped down, and it wasn't a giant at all, but the lady who lived at the edge of the forest and always fed him nuts.

"Don't cry," said the squirrel. "Why are you crying?"

"Because my surprise's gone," said the mother. "I made a beautiful gingerbread rabbit for a surprise for my little girl, and now he's run away, and I've run and I've run and I still can't catch up with him, and now I don't know whether he went to the left or whether he went to the right—I'll never get him back!"

The squirrel didn't know what to say. Finally he said all over again: "Don't cry."

"I can't help it," said the mother. "If you were as disappointed as I am, you'd cry too. It was such a *beautiful* rabbit."

The squirrel said: "He thinks you're going to eat him. To cook him and eat him."

"I made him out of gingerbread," said the mother, "and I was going to bake him in the

oven, but I wouldn't dream of eating him now. I want him to be a pet for my little girl."

"A pet?" said the squirrel.

"Yes," said the mother, "and he can play with her in the daytime and sleep in her room with her every night. I'll make him a little gingerbread house all his own. Oh, squirrel, didn't you see which way he went? Please tell me which way he went."

"I don't know whether it would be right to," the squirrel said.

"Oh, *please* tell me," said the mother, and she gave a big sob. The squirrel just couldn't help himself, he pointed to the right-hand path and said: "He went that way. But promise me you won't eat him!"

"Why, of course I won't eat him," said the mother. "Do you think I'm a *cannibal?*" And after she'd thanked the squirrel she started down the right-hand path as fast as she could go.

In the meantime the rabbit had run along

the path as fast as *he* could go, but in next to no time he was out of breath again. His heart thumped so and he panted so that he said to himself: "I just can't run any more, I've *got* to find some place to hide." Just then at the bottom of a big mossy rock, hidden in the midst of some green bushes, he saw the entrance to a little cave. By it was sitting a beautiful furry red animal with a white breast and a beautiful big plumy red tail. "If only he'd let me hide in his cave," thought the rabbit. So he went up to him and tried to say in a polite voice: "Hello." But he was panting so hard that it sounded just like: "Huh-huh-huh-huh-huh-lo!"

"Ah, good morning, good morning," the other said.

The rabbit said: "I—I—"

"Why, my dear fellow," said the other, "you're completely out of breath. But no wonder—on such an unseasonably warm day as this, a run through the forest is enough to exhaust anyone. Come, sit down here beside me in the shade!"

The rabbit sat down on the bank of moss; he was already beginning to get his breath.

"Now tell me," said the beautiful red animal, "what is there that I can do for you? I can tell from your expression that something is troubling you."

"They—they're going to eat me," the rabbit said. "They're—"

"*Eat* you!" cried the other. "Eat *you!* But who could be guilty of such an enormity? I myself have been, for almost more years than I can remember, a vegetarian; but the thought that even the most confirmed meat-eater could bear to gobble up so young, so innocent, so tender a rabbit as yourself . . ."—he brushed a tear out of his eyes, swallowed, and licked his lips—"the thought is one that—the very thought of it is—why, my dear boy, words fail me!"

"Are you friends with some rabbits your-

self?" asked the rabbit. "Is that how you know I'm a rabbit?"

"Am I friends with some rabbits myself?" repeated the other. He gave a hearty laugh, and waved his paw. "Is that how I know you're a rabbit?" He gave an even heartier laugh, and waved both paws. "Why, my dear fellow, *what do you think I am myself?*"

The rabbit said: "You mean that you—"

"I mean that I'm a rabbit! A red rabbit, I admit. A long-tailed rabbit, I admit. A short-eared rabbit, I admit. But a *rabbit*—and a rabbit that would lay down his life for the sake of a brother rabbit!"

The gingerbread rabbit was so overjoyed that he could hardly speak. Tears came into his eyes, so that the two raisins got bigger and shinier and almost looked like grapes. "To think that at last I've met another rabbit!" he exclaimed.

"But tell me," said the other, "what is it that's trying to eat you? A wolf? A—not a dog,

I hope? I judge from the way that you were running that the scoundrel's not too far behind."

"A giant!" said the gingerbread rabbit. "A giant that's going to cook me alive!"

"To *cook* you!" said the other rabbit. "What an absurd—that is to say, what an atrocious thing to do!"

"Awful, awful!" exclaimed the gingerbread rabbit. "And I can't keep on running, I'm so tired. I've just got to hide. Could I—would you let me hide inside your lovely cave?"

The other smiled, and said cordially: "Why, my dear fellow, I'd be delighted. It's exactly what I was about to propose to you myself. But there was one thing I meant to ask you about this giant of yours. Does it wear a red coat?"

"A red coat?" repeated the rabbit.

"Yes, a red coat. And did it have a lot of noisy dogs with it?"

"Oh, no," said the gingerbread rabbit. "All

it had with it was a lot of paper sacks. It came over to me and picked me up and I could see its terrible big teeth. It had *big* teeth—bigger than yours, even."

"Bigger than mine," said the other thoughtfully. "Yes, my teeth *are* large. All that lettuce and grass, you know—gnaw, gnaw. Well, I expect it's time for us to be getting on into my cave." He smiled and leaned closer to the rabbit.

Just at the moment the rabbit heard, coming down the path, getting nearer and nearer, the sound of footsteps. But it wasn't someone running along heavily like the giant, it was someone hopping lightly and humming to himself, and he was coming from the opposite direction. "What's that?" said the rabbit.

"What *is* that?" said the other, switching his tail. He sounded annoyed. "We'd better jump right into my cave and hide—if you ask me, it's another giant."

"Oh, no!" said the rabbit. "The giant makes

32

a tremendous noise. This one sounds more as if—"

But before he could finish his sentence there came around the corner a rabbit, the biggest, brownest rabbit you ever saw—the very same rabbit the mother had seen at the edge of the forest. "Look!" said the gingerbread rabbit. "A *rabbit!*"

"Quick, quick!" said the other. "Into the cave!"

The gingerbread rabbit said: "Why, we don't need to hide from a rabbit, do we?"

"No, no!" the other cried. "From the giant, the giant! I can hear it coming now." He tugged at the rabbit's arm and started to pull him into the mouth of the cave.

The rabbit couldn't hear anything, but he was terribly frightened just the same. The big brown rabbit came hopping up—he hadn't seen them yet—and the gingerbread rabbit called to him: "The giant will get you! The giant will get you!"

"What? What?" said the big rabbit cheerfully.

"Quick, come hide in the rabbit's hole," cried the gingerbread rabbit.

"In whose hole?" asked the big rabbit.

"In the rabbit's hole! He wants us to," the gingerbread rabbit said.

"In what rabbit's hole?"

"In *his* hole. *His!*" cried the gingerbread rabbit, turning and pointing to the beautiful red rabbit. But the beautiful red rabbit wasn't there. He had disappeared into the hole, and all the rabbit could see or hear was a little soft whisper that came from the mouth of the cave and said: "Come on! Come on! The giant will get you!"

"He's already gone down inside," said the gingerbread rabbit. "Come on! Come on! The giant will get you!"

The big rabbit said in quite a calm voice: "I don't believe in giants. And I don't believe in going in holes, either—not till I've made sure what's inside. You say there's a rabbit in that hole?"

"Oh yes," said the gingerbread rabbit. "A *beautiful* rabbit! Except for me, he's the most beautiful rabbit I've ever seen."

The big rabbit said: "Well, I'm not sure that you're the most beautiful rabbit I've ever seen, but you certainly are the most unusual one. If the other rabbit's that unusual, you're some pair!"

"Oh, he's lots more unusual than I am," said the gingerbread rabbit. "He's covered with the most beautiful red fur, and he's got the longest tail I ever saw, and his teeth are— look how big his teeth are!" For as soon as the gingerbread rabbit had begun to describe him, the beautiful red animal had stuck his head out of the hole and started toward them.

"Fox! Fox!" said the big rabbit. "Run for your life, it's a fox!" He grabbed the gingerbread rabbit by the arm, and the two started off down the path as fast as they could go—

and just two steps behind, his long tail switching and his big teeth shining, came the fox. But the big rabbit could run a lot faster than the fox, and the gingerbread rabbit, now that he'd got all rested again, could run faster than anything—the two of them got farther and farther ahead of the fox, until finally they couldn't even see him or hear him any more.

36

And then they came to a little stream that ran
between the forest and a meadow, and instead
of jumping across, the big brown rabbit said:
"Over here!" They ran along the bank for a
few steps. There at the edge of the water,
under a willow tree with rushes and watercress
growing all around it, was a little shady round

hole. "Do come in," said the big rabbit. "I'd like for you to meet my wife."

The gingerbread rabbit said: "Oh, I'd love to." But then he said in a disappointed voice: "That beautiful red rabbit wasn't a rabbit at all? He told me he was."

"A real rabbit doesn't need to tell you he's a rabbit," said the other. He and the gingerbread rabbit squeezed inside the hole, went down a few steps, and came out into the loveliest little cave you ever saw. The floor of the cave was all covered with shiny white sand— a little light came in from the door and some more light came in from a hole they'd dug in the edge of the bank for a window. Against one wall there were three beds made out of beautiful green rushes and against the other wall there was a little mound of lettuce, and one of carrots, and one of watercress.

"Darling," said the big rabbit, "I'd like for you to meet this new friend I found out in the forest."

"Why, how delightful!" said his wife. She was a silvery gray rabbit and had the most beautiful white tail. "You're the first rabbit we've seen for months and months, you know —the nearest family lives way over on the other side of the forest."

"I'm awfully glad to meet you," said the gingerbread rabbit. "You and your husband are the first rabbits I've ever seen."

"The first rabbits you've ever seen! How can that be?" said the other.

Then the gingerbread rabbit told them all about the kitchen and the mixing bowl and the paring knife and the rolling pin and the giant and the oven and the squirrel and the fox. When he'd finished the big brown rabbit said: "I've never heard anything like it. You're lucky to be alive!"

"You *poor* thing!" said his wife. "How nice that my dear husband found you and brought you here! And now it's time for us all to have our lunch." She went over and put two tiny

golden carrots and a crisp little bunch of watercress on a curly green lettuce leaf. Then she held it out to the gingerbread rabbit.

"I've never really *eaten* anything," he said uncertainly. "I'm only a gingerbread rabbit, you know."

"Just try," she said. "You'll love it."

And when the gingerbread rabbit took a little bite of the watercress it was delicious. Then he took a bite of carrot and a bite of

lettuce, and both of them tasted so good that he took another bite, and another, and another, and didn't even notice the other two rabbits who, while they were eating their own lunch, talked softly to each other. When he'd finished everything that was on his plate and his plate too—because it was a lettuce leaf, you remember—he said to the other two rabbits: "It was just delicious. I've never in all my life tasted anything so good." Then he said: "Well, of course it's the *only* thing I've ever tasted. But I don't see how anything could taste better."

The mother rabbit said: "How would you like to live with us all the time, and always have lettuce and carrots and watercress to eat? And you could sleep in this nice rushy bed here, and go on walks with us in the forest, and go out in the meadow and play hide-and-seek with us at night, and it would be exactly the same as if you were our very own little rabbit. We've always wanted to have a little rabbit of our own, and that's why we made the other little bed here."

The gingerbread rabbit was so happy that tears came into his eyes, and he said: "I'd like to live with you always. Always!"

"Well," said the big brown rabbit, clearing his throat, "that's settled! And now let's all three of us have a nice nap. The moon will be full tonight, you know, and we can go out in the meadow and play all night." Then the big brown rabbit lay down in the right-hand bed, and the silvery gray rabbit lay down in the left-hand bed, and the gingerbread rabbit lay down in the bed in the middle. Then they stretched, and yawned, and said good night to each other, and before they knew it all three of them were fast asleep.

In the meantime the mother had kept walking along the right-hand path. But the big brown rabbit and the gingerbread rabbit had run so fast that the fox never did catch up with them, and of course the mother never did

catch up with them either. But pretty soon she met the fox, who was walking sulkily back to his cave, all out of breath, and she said to him: "Fox, please tell me, have you seen a big brown rabbit?"

"Two of them," said the fox in a very discontented tone of voice.

"*Two* of them!" said the mother surprisedly. "The one I mean's made out of gingerbread."

The fox said: "What's gingerbread?"

"Well," said the mother, "it's what you get when you mix together flour and molasses and brown sugar and ginger, and then bake them all in the oven."

"What does it taste like?" asked the fox. "Meat?"

"Oh, no," said the mother. "It's more like vegetables."

"Vegetables!" exclaimed the fox. "To think that I got all out of breath running after a vegetable!"

"Running after a vegetable?" repeated the mother.

"A fox has got to live too," said the fox in a complacent voice, "and if you ask me, there's nothing better for him to live on than rabbits. Real rabbits, that is—not that vegetable rabbit of yours. Well, he's gone, and the real rabbit's gone too, and you may as well start on home and bake yourself another rabbit. But why don't you bake yourself a real rabbit this time? *That* would be good." And the fox licked his lips.

"I couldn't bear to eat a real rabbit," said the mother. "And after today I couldn't bear to eat a gingerbread rabbit either. Oh dear, I'm *so* disappointed! The rabbit was going to be a surprise for my little girl when she comes home from school."

Said the fox: "Why don't you just hide behind the door and jump out and say *Boo!* at her when she comes in? That would be a real surprise."

"I don't mean that kind of surprise," the mother said, "I mean a nice surprise. I was going to let her have the gingerbread rabbit for a pet, and make a little house for him to sleep in. He was such a *beautiful* rabbit."

When the mother said this it made her think what a beautiful fox the fox was, and she asked him: "How would you like to come home with me and be my little girl's pet?"

The fox looked as if he didn't much like the idea, but he said: "What would you feed me?"

"What would you like?" asked the mother. "Dog food?"

"Dog food!" exclaimed the fox. He shuddered. By then they'd come to his cave, and he said to the mother: "Well, I really must be leaving you. Time for my afternoon nap, you know."

The mother felt so discouraged that she gave a little sob, and said to the fox: "Please help me think of a surprise for my little girl. Everybody says foxes are so clever!"

"So they are," said the fox. "Well, in *my* experience there's no surprise that children enjoy so much as a nice bone." And without so much as saying good-by to the mother, he popped into his hole.

So the mother walked slowly along toward home, feeling very sad. Pretty soon she came to the big oak tree. The squirrel was sitting on the branch outside his nest, and he called down to the mother: "Did you find him?"

"No," said the mother, "he's gone for good. And now my little girl will come home and there'll be no surprise for her."

The squirrel said: "Have you thought of giving her some nuts? Children love nuts."

"Oh, a nut's not a *surprise*," the mother said. "I want a real surprise for her, one like that beautiful gingerbread rabbit."

"Well, why don't you make her another rabbit?" suggested the squirrel. "You could make it out of—"

All at once the mother clapped her hands together, jumped up in the air, and made a noise that sounded like a rabbit squealing, she was so overjoyed. "I *will* make her another

rabbit," she cried. "I'll make one that looks exactly like the gingerbread rabbit, only this time I'll make it out of brown felt, and stuff it with cotton, and use a red button for its mouth, a white button for its nose, and two shiny black buttons for its eyes. Oh, thank you so much, squirrel! Thank you, thank you!"

The mother was so excited that she forgot to say good-by to the squirrel, even, but started home as fast as her legs would carry her. The minute she got there she got out her sewing basket and a big piece of brown felt and some cotton she used to stuff quilts with. She cut out two pieces of felt exactly like the front and the back of the gingerbread rabbit, sewed them together on the sewing machine, and stuffed them full of cotton.

Then she sewed on the buttons for the rabbit's mouth and nose and eyes, and lined the inside of the rabbit's ears with pink silk, so that he looked even more like a real rabbit than the gingerbread rabbit did. She hadn't even had time to stop for lunch, she worked so hard and sewed so fast.

Just as she finished sewing the pink silk inside the rabbit's ears, she heard her little Mary's voice in the front yard. She ran to the front door, opened it, and stood the rabbit up between the door and the wall. When her little girl came in and they'd both said hello and kissed each other, the mother said to her: "Surprise!"

"What?" said the little girl. "Where?"

"Right in this room," said the mother. Then the little girl looked all around, but she couldn't see anything. She looked inside the fireplace and under the sofa, and finally when she got near the door the mother said: "You're warm," and the little girl ran and looked behind the door and—there was the rabbit!

"Oh, it's just *beautiful*, Mother," the little girl said. "It's the best surprise I've ever had in

my whole life. He looks *exactly* like a ginger-bread rabbit."

"He does look like one, doesn't he?" the mother said.

"He looks very like a real rabbit, too," said the little girl. "If I just saw him out in the yard and went up to him I'd expect him to run right off into the forest."

"Oh *no!*" said the mother. "He wouldn't do that. Surely he wouldn't do *that!*"

And he never did. In the afternoon when the little girl came home from school she'd take him with her wherever she went, and at night she'd take him to bed with her.

And at night when the little girl and her mother were fast asleep, sometimes the big brown rabbit and the silvery gray rabbit and the gingerbread rabbit would come to the edge of the forest, on their way to some lovely lettuce patch or carrot patch or turnip patch, and they'd look at the house, all sleeping in the moonlight, and the gingerbread rabbit would say: "That's where the giant lives. Oh, those teeth! Did she almost cook me! Did she almost eat me!"

And the other two rabbits were too polite to tell him that it wasn't a giant at all, but just a mother and her little girl; they'd smile and pat him, and all three of them would say: "Good-by, old giant!" and run off into the forest.